Families Are Funny

by Nan Hunt

illustrated by
Deborah Niland

Orchard Books
New York

First American Edition 1992 published by Orchard Books
First published in Australia by William Collins Pty. Ltd.
in association with Anne Ingram Books

Orchard Books
387 Park Avenue South
New York, NY 10016

Manufactured in the United States of America
Printed by Barton Press, Inc.
Bound by Horowitz/Rae
Book design by Susan Phillips

10 9 8 7 6 5 4 3 2 1

The text of this book is set in 16 point Novarese Medium.

Library of Congress Cataloging-in-Publication Data
Hunt, Nan.
Families are funny / by Nan Hunt ; illustrated by Deborah Niland.—1st American ed.
p. cm.
"First published by William Collins Pty. Ltd., Australia, in association with Anne Ingram Books"—T.p. verso.
Summary: Families often do odd and irritating things, but a little boy discovers they're there if you need them.
ISBN 0-531-05969-3. — ISBN 0-531-08569-4 (lib. bdg.)
[1. Family—Fiction.] I. Niland, Deborah, ill. II. Title. PZ7.H91624Fam 1992
[E]—dc20 91-15628

For mine, bless them

—N.H.

For Mum, with love

—D.N.

Families are funny.
When Dad calls me, he says,
"I want you this minute. Move it!"

But when I want him, he says,
"Not now. Can't you see I'm busy?"

Mom's just as bad. If there is something exciting on television, or a big butterfly floating around the garden—something I know she would love to see—and I yell, "Mom, Mom! Come quickly!" what does she say?

"In a minute."
By the time she comes, it is always too late.

My sister Jasmine and her friends lock themselves in her room.
"Let me in!" I shout.
"Go away!" she screams.
But if Grandma gives me a bag of candy, Jasmine is all over me like a rash.

My brother Dave is teaching me to play cricket.
He plays with me until his friends come over.
Then he says, "Beat it."

Grandpa was once a football star, but he's funny now. Just when I'm about to make a touchdown, he'll say, "That's enough. Time out."

Grandma is funny, too. Sometimes she's all lovey-dovey, but at other times she sniffs at me and says, "I don't know why your parents allow such behavior. Things were certainly different in my day."

When Uncle Jack visits, he always says, "Well, kid, what do you want to do?" Then we do what he wants to do.

My aunt Rose is gorgeous. Her clothes are all bright colors, and she smells wonderful. She says the most outrageous things, and nobody seems to mind. But when I am sweaty from playing outside and try to hug her, she says, "Hi, Batman. Why don't you go play in traffic?"

My great-grandmother is very old. She wears a wig. I saw her once when she didn't have it on. She was nearly bald, with a few wispy white hairs. She caught me staring at her and roared with laughter.

"I think I'll get a blonde wig next year," she told me.
"How would you like that?"
"I like you the way you are," I said.

We have relatives called once-removed and twice-removed cousins. Cousin Alf was once removed from our house in a hurry after he put chewing gum all over the cat's fur. Dad says Cousin Julia is twice removed. I wonder what *she* did?

One day I woke up feeling funny. My head was going BOOM, BOOM, like a bass drum, and my whole body was hot and sore.

The doctor came and felt my head. He listened to my chest and looked for spots. He poked me all over. I felt awful.

Dad checked on me all the time. He'd come in and say, "Hi. Is there anything I can do for you?"

Mom was never very faraway.

My brother and my sister treated me as
if I belonged to an endangered species.
My grandparents and great-grandparents
and uncles and aunts and cousins sent
cards and came to see me. They brought
wonderful presents and all kinds of fruit.

Families sure are funny.
But when I was sick, I learned...

they are the very *best* people to have around.